Former RAF pilot and investigative journalist, **Frederick Forsyth** defined the modern thriller when he wrote *The Day of The Jackal*, with its lightning-paced storytelling, effortlessly cool reality and unique insider information. Since then he has written eleven further bestselling novels. He lives in England.

. . . .

THE DAY OF THE JACKAL

An anonymous Englishman is hired to assassinate the French president, General Charles de Gaulle.

'In a class by itself. Unputdownable'
Sunday Times

◆

THE ODESSA FILE

The discovery of the diary of a former concentration camp survivor triggers a life and death hunt for a notorious Nazi war criminal.

'Brilliant entertainment and a disquieting book'
Guardian

◆

THE DOGS OF WAR

The discovery of platinum in a remote African republic changes the rules in a power game where the stakes have become terrifyingly high.

'One of the world's best thriller writers'
Wall Street Journal

THE DEVIL'S ALTERNATIVE

'Whichever option I choose, men are going to die.' The US President faces an appalling choice which will decide the fates of many.

'Compulsively readable...I was hypnotised'
Financial Times

◆

THE FOURTH PROTOCOL

A lone MI5 investigator leads an operation to stop an act of murderous devastation aimed at pitching Britain into revolution.

'A triumph of plot, construction and research'
The Times

◆

THE NEGOTIATOR

The world's foremost negotiator, who must bargain for the life of an innocent man, unaware that ransom was never the kidnapper's real objective.

'Intricately plotted, fast moving and full of surprises'
Evening Standard

◆

THE DECEIVER

At the end of the Cold War, the career of one Special Intelligence Service officer hangs in the balance.

'Another Forsyth thriller that has you by the throat with plots so finely crafted as to make the cold war's very darkness visible'
Daily Mail

THE FIST OF GOD

As Saddam Hussein prepares to invade Kuwait, his most terrifying weapon must be destroyed before it can decimate the Allied forces.

'Forsyth's expertise and research lend the book a powerful ring of authenticity and he has an almost mesmeric ability to compel the reader to keep turning the page. It's a corking good read'

Spectator

ICON

A terrifying secret document smuggled out of Russia precipitates a desperate mission into one of the world's most anarchic cities, Moscow.

'Forsyth's narrative surges along with great power; the story is terrifying and timely...Komarov grips you to the end'

Daily Telegraph

AVENGER

A billionaire unleashes a Special Forces loner to avenge the brutal murder of his grandson.

'Forsyth's storytelling mastery goes from strength to strength. Don't imagine you know what's going to happen next. Forsyth delivers a brilliant finale and a twist that'll make your head spin'

Daily Mirror

THE AFGHAN

A Westerner must achieve the impossible and pass
himself off as an Arab among Arabs to foil a plot which
will destroy world peace.

'Wedding a superb command of detail to a story
of pace and power, Forsyth has written a counter-
terrorism primer-thriller of chilling relevance'

Observer

THE COBRA

The world's most deadly trade, the cocaine industry,
must be destroyed – by any means necessary.

'When it comes to espionage, international intrigue
and suspense, Frederick Forsyth is a master'

Washington Post

ALSO BY
FREDERICK FORSYTH

THE BIAFRA STORY

GREAT FLYING STORIES

NO COMEBACKS

THE VETERAN

THE SHEPHERD

THE PHANTOM OF MANHATTAN

THE SHEPHERD

Frederick Forsyth

arrow books

Reissued by Arrow Books 2011

2 4 6 8 10 9 7 5 3 1

First published in Great Britain in 1975 by Hutchinson

Arrow Books
The Random House Group Limited
20 Vauxhall Bridge Road, London SW1V 2SA

Addresses for companies within The Random House Group Limited can
be found at: www.randomhouse.co.uk/offices.htm

The Random House Group Limited Reg. No. 954009

www.rbooks.co.uk

A CIP catalogue record for this book
is available from the British Library

ISBN 9780099559863

The Random House Group Limited supports The Forest Stewardship

Council (FSC), the leading international forest certification organisation.
All our titles that are printed on Greenpeace approved FSC certified paper
carry the FSC logo. Our paper procurement policy can be found at:
www.rbooks.co.uk/environment

Printed and bound in Great Britain by
CPI Cox & Wyman, Reading, RG1 8EX

For my darling wife Carole

The Shepherd

For a brief moment, while waiting for the
control tower to clear me for takeoff, I glanced
out through the Perspex cockpit canopy at the
surrounding German countryside. It lay white and
crisp beneath the crackling December moon.

Behind me lay the boundary fence of the Royal
Air Force base, and beyond the fence, as I had seen
while swinging my little fighter into line with the
takeoff runway, the sheet of snow covering the flat
farmland stretched away to the line of the pine
trees, two miles distant in the night yet so clear I
could almost see the shapes of the trees themselves.

Ahead of me, as I waited for the voice of the
controller to come through the headphones, was
the runway itself, a slick black ribbon of tarmac,
flanked by twin rows of bright-burning lights,
illuminating the solid path cut earlier by the
snowplows. Behind the lights were the humped
banks of the morning's snow, frozen hard once
again where the snowplow blades had pushed
them. Far away to my right, the airfield tower stood
up like a single glowing candle amid the brilliant
hangars where the muffled aircraftmen were even
now closing down the station for the night.

Inside the control tower, I knew, all was warmth
and merriment, the staff waiting only for my
departure to close down also, jump into the waiting

cars, and head back to the parties in the mess. Within minutes of my going, the lights would die out, leaving only the huddled hangars, seeming hunched against the bitter night, the shrouded fighter planes, the sleeping fuel-bowser trucks, and, above them all, the single flickering station light, brilliant red above the black-and-white airfield, beating out in Morse code the name of the station—CELLE—to an unheeding sky. For tonight there would be no wandering aviators to look down and check their bearings; tonight was Christmas Eve, in the year of grace 1957, and I was a young pilot trying to get home to Blighty for his Christmas leave.

I was in a hurry and my watch read ten-fifteen by the dim blue glow of the control panel where the rows of dials quivered and danced. It was warm and snug inside the cockpit, the heating turned up full to prevent the Perspex' icing up. It was like a cocoon, small and warm and safe, shielding me from the bitter cold outside, from the freezing night that can kill a man inside a minute if he is exposed to it at six hundred miles an hour.

"Charlie Delta…"

The controller's voice woke me from my reverie, sounding in my headphones as if he were with me in the tiny cockpit, shouting in my ear. He's had a jar or two already, I thought. Strictly against orders, but what the hell? It's Christmas Eve.

"Charlie Delta…Control," I responded.

"Charlie Delta, clear takeoff," he said.

I saw no point in responding. I simply eased the throttle forward slowly with the left hand, holding the Vampire steady down the central line with the right hand. Behind me the low whine of the Goblin engine rose and rose, passing through a cry and into a scream. The snub-nosed fighter rolled, the lights each side of the runway passed in ever quicker succession, till they were flashing in a continuous blur. She became light, the nose rose fractionally, freeing the nosewheel from contact with the runway, and the rumble vanished instantly. Seconds later the main wheels came away and their soft drumming also stopped. I held her low above the deck, letting the speed build up till a glance at the air-speed indicator told me we were through 120 knots and heading for 150. As the end of the runway whizzed beneath my feet I pulled the Vampire into a gently climbing turn to the left, easing up the undercarriage lever as I did so.

From beneath and behind me I heard the dull clunk of the wheels entering their bays and felt the lunge forward of the jet as the drag of the under-carriage vanished. In front of me the three red lights representing three wheels extinguished themselves. I held her into the climbing turn, pressing the radio button with the left thumb.

"Charlie Delta, clear airfield, wheels up and locked," I said into my oxygen mask.

"Charlie Delta, roger, over to Channel D," said the controller, and then, before I could change radio channels, he added, "Happy Christmas."

Strictly against the rules of radio procedure, of course. I was very young then, and very conscientious. But I replied, "Thank you, Tower, and same to you." Then I switched channels to tune into the RAF's North Germany Air Control frequency.

Down on my right thigh was strapped the map with my course charted on it in blue ink, but I did not need it. I knew the details by heart, worked out earlier with the navigation officer in the nav. hut. Turn overhead Celle airfield onto course 265 degrees, continue climbing to 27,000 feet. On reaching height, maintain course and keep speed to 485 knots. Check in with Channel D to let them know you're in their airspace, then a straight run over the Dutch coast south of the Bevelands into the North Sea. After forty-four minutes' flying time, change to Channel F and call Lakenheath Control to give you a "steer." Fourteen minutes later you'll be overhead Lakenheath. After that, follow instructions and they'll bring you down on a radio-controlled descent. No problem, all routine procedures. Sixty-six minutes' flying time, with the descent and landing, and the Vampire had enough fuel for over eighty minutes in the air.

Swinging over Celle airfield at 5,000 feet, I straightened up and watched the needle on my compass settle happily down on a course of 265 degrees. The nose was pointing toward the black, freezing vault of the night sky, studded with stars so brilliant they flickered their white fire against the eyeballs. Below, the black-and-white map of north Germany was growing smaller, the dark masses of the pine forests blending into the white expanses of the fields. Here and there a village or small town glittered with lights. Down there amid the gaily lit streets the carol singers would be out, knocking on the holly-studded doors to sing "Silent Night" and collect *pfennigs* for charity. The Westphalian housewives would be preparing hams and geese.

Four hundred miles ahead of me the story would be the same, the carols in my own language but many of the tunes the same, and it would be turkey instead of goose. But whether you call it *Weihnacht* or Christmas, it's the same all over the Christian world, and it was good to be going home.

From Lakenheath I knew I could get a lift down

to London in the liberty bus, leaving just after midnight; from London I was confident I could hitch a lift to my parents' home in Kent. By breakfast time I'd be celebrating with my own family. The altimeter read 27,000 feet. I eased the nose forward, reduced throttle setting to give me an air speed of 485 knots and held her steady on 265 degrees. Somewhere beneath me in the gloom the Dutch border would be slipping away, and I had been airborne for twenty-one minutes. No problem.

The problem started ten minutes out over the North Sea, and it started so quietly that it was several minutes before I realized I had one at all.

For some time I had been unaware that the low hum coming through my headphones into my ears had ceased, to be replaced by the strange nothingness of total silence. I must have been failing to concentrate, my thoughts being of home and my waiting family. The first thing I knew was when I flicked a glance downward to check my course on the compass. Instead of being rock-steady on 265 degrees, the needle was drifting lazily round the clock, passing through east, west, south, and north with total impartiality.

I swore a most unseasonal sentiment against the compass and the instrument fitter who should have

checked it for 100-percent reliability. Compass failure at night, even a brilliant moonlit night such as the one beyond the cockpit Perspex, was no fun. Still, it was not too serious: there was a standby compass—the alcohol kind. But, when I glanced at it, that one seemed to be in trouble, too. The needle was swinging wildly. Apparently something had jarred the case—which isn't uncommon. In any event, I could call up Lakenheath in a few minutes and they would give me a GCA—Ground Controlled Approach—the second-by-second instructions that a well-equipped airfield can give a pilot to bring him home in the worst of weathers, following his progress on ultraprecise radar screens, watching him descend all the way to the tarmac, tracing his position in the sky yard by yard and second by second. I glanced at my watch: thirty-four minutes airborne. I could try to raise Lakenheath now, at the outside limit of my radio range.

Before trying Lakenheath, the correct procedure would be to inform Channel D, to which I was tuned, of my little problem, so they could advise Lakenheath that I was on my way without a compass. I pressed the TRANSMIT button and called:

"Celle, Charlie Delta, Celle, Charlie Delta, calling North Beveland Control...."

I stopped. There was no point in going on. Instead of the lively crackle of static and the sharp

sound of my own voice coming back into my own ears, there was a muffled murmur inside my oxygen mask. My own voice speaking...and going nowhere. I tried again. Same result. Far back across the wastes of the black and bitter North Sea, in the warm, cheery concrete complex of North Beveland Control, men sat back from their control panel, chatting and sipping their steaming coffee and cocoa. And they could not hear me. The radio was dead.

Fighting down the rising sense of panic that can kill a pilot faster than anything else, I swallowed and slowly counted to ten. Then I switched to

Channel F and tried to raise Lakenheath, ahead of me amid the Suffolk countryside, lying in its forest of pine trees south of Thetford, beautifully equipped with its GCA system for bringing home lost aircraft. On Channel F the radio was as dead as ever. My own muttering into the oxygen mask was smothered by the surrounding rubber. The steady whistle of my own jet engine behind me was my only answer.

It's a very lonely place, the sky, and even more so the sky on a winter's night. And a single-seater jet fighter is a lonely home, a tiny steel box held aloft on stubby wings, hurled through the freezing

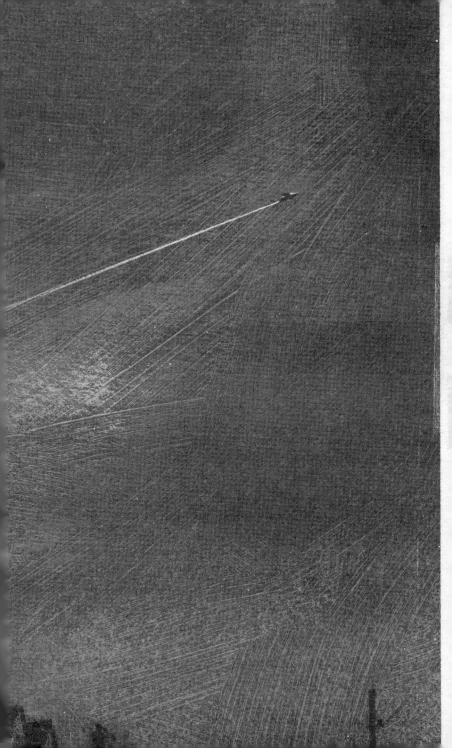

emptiness by a blazing tube throwing out the strength of six thousand horses every second. But the loneliness is offset, canceled out, by the knowledge that at the touch of a button on the throttle, the pilot can talk to other human beings, people who care about him, men and women who staff a network of stations around the world; just one touch of that button, the TRANSMIT button, and scores of them in control towers across the land that are tuned to his channel can hear him call for help. When the pilot transmits, on every one of those screens a line of light streaks from the center of the screen to the outside rim, which is marked with

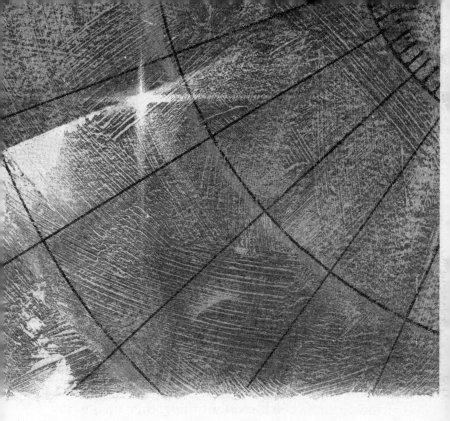

figures, from one to three hundred and sixty. Where the streak of light hits the ring, that is where the aircraft lies in relation to the control tower listening to him. The control towers are linked, so with two cross bearings they can locate his position to within a few hundred yards. He is not lost any more. People begin working to bring him down.

The radar operators pick up the little dot he makes on their screens from all the other dots; they call him up and give him instructions. "Begin your descent now, Charlie Delta. We have you now...." Warm, experienced voices, voices which control an array of electronic devices that can reach out across the winter sky, through the ice and rain, above the snow and cloud, to pluck the lost one from his deadly infinity and bring him down to the flare-lit runway that means home and life itself.

When the pilot transmits. But for that he must have a radio. Before I had finished testing Channel J, the international emergency channel, and obtained the same negative result, I knew my ten-channel radio set was as dead as the dodo.

It had taken the RAF two years to train me to fly their fighters for them, and most of that time had been spent in training precisely for emergency procedures. The important thing, they used to say in flying school, is not to know how to fly in perfect conditions; it is to fly through an emergency and stay alive. Now the training was beginning to take effect.

While I was vainly testing my radio channels, my eyes scanned the instrument panel in front of me. The instruments told their own message. It was no coincidence the compass and the radio had failed together; both worked off the aircraft's electrical circuits. Somewhere beneath my feet, amid the miles of brightly colored wiring that make up the circuits, there had been a main fuse blowout. I reminded myself, idiotically, to forgive the instrument fitter and blame the electrician. Then I took stock of the nature of my disaster.

The first thing to do in such a case, I remembered old Flight Sergeant Norris telling us, is to reduce throttle setting from cruise speed to a slower setting, to give maximum flight endurance.

"We don't want to waste valuable fuel, do we, gentlemen? We might need it later. So we reduce the power setting from 10,000 revolutions per minute to 7,200. That way we will fly a little slower, but we will stay in the air rather longer, won't we, gentlemen?" He always referred to us all being in the same emergency at the same time, did Sergeant Norris. I eased the throttle back and watched the rev counter. It operates on its own generator and so I

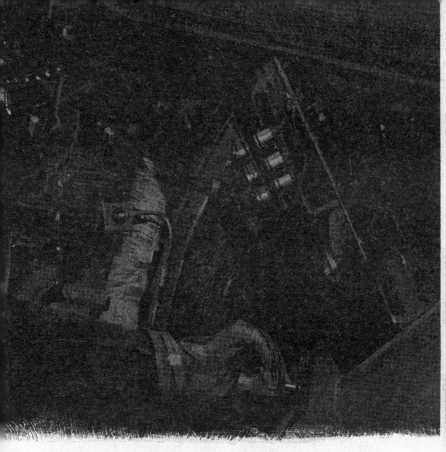

hadn't lost that, at least. I waited until the Goblin was turning over at about 7,200 rpm, and felt the aircraft slow down. The nose rose fractionally, so I adjusted the flight trim to keep her straight and level.

The main instruments in front of a pilot's eyes are six, including the compass. The five others are the air-speed indicator, the altimeter, the vertical-speed indicator, the bank indicator (which tells him if he's banking, i.e., turning, to left or right), and the slip indicator (which tells him if he's skidding crabwise across the sky). Two of these are electrically operated, and they had gone the same way as my compass. That left me with the three pressure-operated instruments—air-speed indicator, altimeter and vertical-speed indicator. In other words, I knew how fast I was going, how high I was and if I were diving or climbing.

It is perfectly possible to land an aircraft with only these three instruments, judging the rest by those old navigational aids, the human eyes. Possible, that is, in conditions of brilliant weather, by daylight and with no cloud in the sky. It is possible, just possible, though not advisable, to try to navigate a fast-moving jet by dead reckoning, using the eyes, looking down and identifying the curve of the coast where it makes an easily recognizable pattern, spotting a strange-shaped reservoir, the glint of a river that the map strapped to the thigh says can only be the Ouse, or the Trent, or the Thames. From lower down it is possible to differentiate Norwich Cathedral tower from Lincoln Cathedral tower, if you know the countryside intimately. By night it is not possible.

The only things that show up at night, even on a bright moonlit night, are the lights. These have patterns when seen from the sky. Manchester looks different from Birmingham; Southampton can be recognized from the shape of its massive harbor and the Solent, cut out in black (the sea shows up black)

against the carpet of the city's lights. I knew Norwich very well, and if I could identify the great curving bulge of the Norfolk coast line from Lowestoft, round through Yarmouth to Cromer, I could find Norwich, the only major sprawl of lights set twenty miles inland from all points on the coast. Five miles north of Norwich, I knew, was the fighter airfield of Merriam St. George, whose red indicator beacon would be blipping out its Morse identification signal into the night. There, if they only had the sense to switch on the airfield lights when they heard me screaming at low level up and down the airfield, I could land safely.

I began to let the Vampire down slowly toward the oncoming coast, my mind feverishly working out how far behind schedule I was through the reduced speed. My watch told me forty-three minutes airborne. The coast of Norfolk had to be somewhere ahead of my nose, five miles below. I glanced up at the full moon, like a searchlight in the glittering sky, and thanked her for her presence.

As the fighter slipped toward Norfolk the sense of loneliness gripped me tighter and tighter. All those things that had seemed so beautiful as I climbed away from the airfield in Lower Saxony now seemed my worst enemies. The stars were no longer impressive in their brilliance; I thought of their hostility, sparkling away there in the timeless, lost infinities of endless space. The night sky, its stratospheric temperature fixed, night and day alike, at an unchanging fifty-six degrees below zero, became in my mind a limitless prison creaking with the cold. Below me lay the worst of them all, the heavy brutality of the North Sea, waiting to swallow up me and my plane and bury us for endless eternity in a liquid black crypt where nothing moved nor would ever move again. And no one would ever know.

At 15,000 feet and still diving, I began to realize that a fresh, and for me the last, enemy had entered the field. There was no ink-black sea three miles below me, no necklace of twinkling seaside lights somewhere up ahead. Far away, to right and left, ahead and no doubt behind me, the light of the moon reflected on a flat and endless sea of white. Perhaps only a hundred, two hundred feet thick, but enough. Enough to blot out all vision, enough to kill me. The East Anglian fog had moved in.

As I had flown westward from Germany, a slight breeze, unforeseen by the weathermen, had sprung up, blowing from the North Sea toward Norfolk. During the previous day the flat, open ground of East Anglia had been frozen hard by the wind and the subzero temperatures. During the evening the

wind had moved a belt of slightly warmer air off the North Sea and onto the plains of East Anglia.

There, coming in contact with the ice-cold earth, the trillions of tiny moisture particles in the sea air had vaporized, forming the kind of fog that can blot out five counties in a matter of thirty minutes. How far westward it stretched I could not tell; to the West Midlands, perhaps, nudging up against the eastern slopes of the Pennines? There was no question of trying to overfly the fog to the westward; without navigational aids or radio, I would be lost over strange, unfamiliar country. Also out of the question was to try to fly back to Holland, to

land at one of the Dutch Air Force bases along the coast there; I had not the fuel. Relying only on my eyes to guide me, it was a question of landing at Merriam St. George or dying amid the wreckage of the Vampire somewhere in the fog-wreathed fens of Norfolk.

At 10,000 feet I pulled out of my dive, increasing power slightly to keep myself airborne, using up more of my precious fuel. Still a creature of my training, I recalled again the instructions of Flight Sergeant Norris:

"When we are totally lost above unbroken cloud, gentlemen, we must consider the necessity of bail-

ing out of our aircraft, must we not?"

Of course, Sergeant. Unfortunately, the Martin Baker ejector seat cannot be fitted to the single-seat Vampire, which is notorious for being almost impossible to bail out of; the only two successful candidates living lost their legs in the process. Still, there has to be a lucky one. What else, Sergeant?

"Our first move, therefore, is to turn our aircraft toward the open sea, away from all areas of intense human habitation."

You mean towns, Sergeant. Those people down there pay for us to fly for them, not to drop a screaming monster of ten tons of steel on top of them on Christmas Eve. There are kids down there, schools, hospitals, homes. You turn your aircraft out to sea.

The procedures were all worked out. They did not mention that the chances of a pilot, bobbing about on a winter's night in the North Sea, frozen face lashed by a subzero wind, supported by a yellow life jacket, ice encrusting his lips, eyebrows, ears, his position unknown by the men sipping their Christmas punches in warm rooms three hundred miles away—that his chances were less than one in a hundred of living longer than one hour. In the training films, they showed you pictures of happy fellows who had announced by radio that they were

ditching, being picked up by helicopters within minutes, and all on a bright, warm summer's day.

"One last procedure, gentlemen, to be used in extreme emergency."

That's better, Sergeant Norris, that's what I'm in now.

"All haircraft happroaching Britain's coasts are visible on the radar scanners of our early-warning system. If, therefore, we have lost our radio and cannot transmit our emergency, we try to attract the attention of our radar scanners by adopting an odd form of behavior. We do this by moving out to sea, then flying in small triangles, turning left, left

and left again, each leg of the triangle being of a duration of two minutes' flying time. In this way we hope to attract attention. When we have been spotted, the air-traffic controller is informed and he diverts another aircraft to find us. This other aircraft, of course, has a radio. When discovered by the rescue aircraft, we formate on him and he brings us down through the cloud or fog to a safe landing."

Yes, it was the last attempt to save one's life. I recalled the details better now. The rescue aircraft which would lead you back to a safe landing, flying wing tip to wing tip, was called the shepherd. I

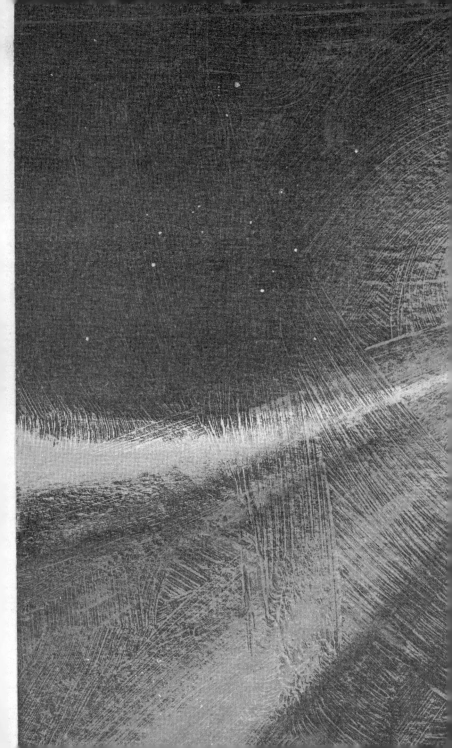

glanced at my watch; fifty-one minutes airborne, about thirty minutes left of fuel. Then I looked at the fuel gauge and saw that I'd lost it along with the rest when the fuse blew. I had an icy moment until I remembered the worry button—which I could press to get an approximate reading. The fuel gauge read one-third full. Knowing myself to be still short of the Norfolk coast, and flying level at 10,000 feet in the moonlight, I pulled the Vampire into a left-hand turn and began my first leg of the first triangle. After two minutes, I pulled left again. Below me, the fog reached back as far as I could see, and ahead of me, toward Norfolk, it was the same.

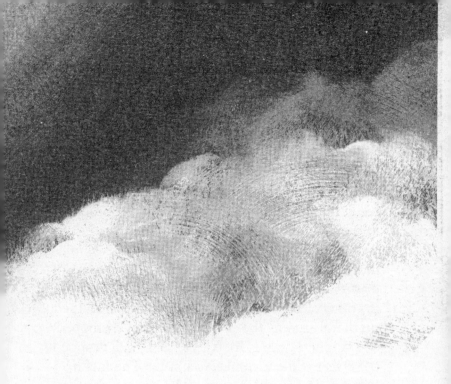

Ten minutes went by, nearly two complete triangles. I had not prayed, not really prayed, for many years, and the habit came hard. Lord, please get me out of this bloody mess....No, you mustn't talk like that to Him. "Our Father, which art in Heaven..." He'd heard that a thousand times, would be hearing it another thousand times tonight. What do you say to Him when you want help? Please, God, make somebody notice me up here; please make someone see me flying in triangles and send up a shepherd to help me down to a safe landing. Please help me, and I promise— What on earth could I promise Him? He had no need of me, and I, who now had need of Him, had taken no notice of Him for so long He'd probably forgotten all about me.

When I had been airborne for seventy-two minutes, I knew no one would come. The compass still drifted aimlessly through all the points of the circle, the other electrical instruments were dead, all their needles frozen at the point where they'd stopped. My altimeter read 7,000 feet, so I had dropped 3,000 feet while turning. No matter. The fuel read between zero and a quarter full—say ten minutes' more flying time. I felt the rage of despair welling up. I began screaming into the dead microphone:

"You stupid bastards, why don't you look at your radar screens? Why can't somebody see me up here? All so damn drunk you can't do your jobs properly. Oh, God, why won't somebody listen to me?" By then the anger had subsided and I had taken to blubbering like a baby from the sheer helplessness of it all.

Five minutes later, I knew, without any doubt of it, that I was going to die that night. Strangely I wasn't even afraid any more. Just enormously sad. Sad for all the things I would never do, the places I would never see, the people I would never greet again. It's a bad thing, a sad thing, to die at twenty years of age with your life unlived, and the worst

thing of all is not the fact of dying but the fact of all the things never done.

Out through the Perspex I could see that the moon was setting, hovering above the horizon of thick white fog; in another two minutes the night sky would be plunged into total darkness and a few minutes later, I would have to bail out of a dying aircraft before it flicked over on its last dive into the North Sea. An hour later I would be dead also, bobbing around in the water, a bright-yellow Mae West supporting a stiff, frozen body. I dropped the left wing of the Vampire toward the moon to bring the aircraft onto the final leg of the last triangle.

Down below the wing tip, against the sheen of the fog bank, up-moon of me, a black shadow crossed the whiteness. For a second I thought it was my own shadow, but with the moon up there, my own shadow would be behind me. It was another aircraft, low against the fog bank, keeping station with me through my turn, a mile down through the sky toward the fog.

The other aircraft being below me, I kept turning, wing down, to keep it in sight. The other aircraft also kept turning, until the two of us had done one complete circle. Only then did I realize why it was so far below me, why he did not climb to my height and take up station on my wing tip. He was flying slower than I; he could not keep up if he tried to fly beside me. Trying hard not to believe he was just another aircraft, moving on his way, about to disappear forever into the fog bank, I eased the throttle back and began to slip down toward him. He kept turning; so did I. At 5,000 feet I knew I was still going too fast for him. I could not reduce power any more for fear of stalling the Vampire and plunging down out of control. To slow up even more, I put out the air brakes. The Vampire shuddered as the brakes swung into the slipstream, slowing the Vampire down to 280 knots.

And then he came up toward me, swinging in toward my left-hand wing tip. I could make out the black bulk of him against the dim white sheet of fog below; then he was with me, a hundred feet off my wing tip, and we straightened out together, rocking as we tried to keep formation. The moon was to my right, and my own shadow masked his shape and form; but even so, I could make out the shimmer of two propellers whirling through the sky ahead of him. Of course, he could not fly at my speed; I was in a jet fighter, he in a piston-engined aircraft of an earlier generation.

He held station alongside me for a few seconds, down-moon of me, half invisible, then banked

gently to the left. I followed, keeping formation with him, for he was obviously the shepherd sent up to bring me down, and he had the compass and the radio, not I. He swung through 180 degrees, then straightened up, flying straight and level, the moon behind him. From the position of the dying moon I knew we were heading back toward the Norfolk coast, and for the first time I could see him well. To my surprise, my shepherd was a De Havilland Mosquito, a fighter bomber of Second World War vintage.

Then I remembered that the Meteorological Squadron at Gloucester used Mosquitoes, the last ones flying, to take samples of the upper atmosphere to help in the preparation of weather forecasts. I had seen them at Battle of Britain displays, flying their Mosquitoes in the flypasts, attracting gasps from the crowd and a few nostalgic shakes of the head from the older men, such as they always reserved on September 15 for the Spitfires, Hurricanes and Lancasters.

Inside the cockpit of the Mosquito I could make out, against the light of the moon, the muffled head of its pilot and the twin circles of his goggles as he looked out the side window toward me. Carefully, he raised his right hand till I could see it in the window, fingers straight, palm downward. He jabbed the fingers forward and down, meaning, "We are going to descend; formate on me."

I nodded and quickly brought up my own left hand so he could see it, pointing forward to my own control panel with one forefinger, then holding up five splayed fingers. Finally, I drew my hand across my throat. By common agreement this sign means I have only five minutes' fuel left, then my engine cuts out. I saw the muffled, goggled, oxygen-masked head nod in understanding, then we were heading downward toward the sheet of fog. His speed increased and I brought the air brakes back in. The Vampire stopped trembling and plunged ahead of the Mosquito. I pulled back on the throttle, hearing the engine die to a low whistle, and the shepherd was back beside me. We were diving straight toward the shrouded land of Norfolk. I glanced at my altimeter: 2,000 feet, still diving.

He pulled out at three hundred feet; the fog was still below us. Probably the fog bank was only from the ground to one hundred feet up, but that was more than enough to prevent a plane from landing without a GCA. I could imagine the stream of instructions coming from the radar hut into the earphones of the man flying beside me, eighty feet away through two panes of Perspex and the wind-stream of icy air moving between us at 280 knots. I

kept my eyes on him, formating as closely as possible, afraid of losing sight for an instant, watching for his every hand signal. Against the white fog, even as the moon sank, I had to marvel at the beauty of his aircraft; the short nose and bubble cockpit, the blister of Perspex right in the nose itself, the long, lean, underslung engine pods, each housing a Rolls-Royce Merlin engine, a masterpiece of craftsmanship, snarling through the night toward home. Two minutes later he held up his clenched left fist in the window, then opened the fist to splay all five fingers against the glass. "Please lower your undercarriage." I moved the lever downward and

felt the dull thunk as all three wheels went down, happily powered by hydraulic pressure and not dependent on the failed electrical system.

The pilot of the shepherd aircraft pointed down again, for another descent, and as he jinked in the moonlight I caught sight of the nose of the Mosquito. It had the letters JK painted on it, large and black. Probably for call sign Jig King. Then we were descending again, more gently this time.

He leveled out just above the fog layer, so low the tendrils of candy floss were lashing at our fuselages, and we went into a steady circular turn. I managed to flick a glance at my fuel gauge; it was on zero,

flickering feebly. For God's sake, hurry up, I prayed, for if my fuel failed me now, there would be no time to climb to the minimum seven hundred feet needed for bailing out. A jet fighter at one hundred feet without an engine is a death trap with no chance for survival.

For two or three minutes he seemed content to hold his slow circular turn, while the sweat broke out behind my neck and began to run in streams down my back, gumming the light nylon flying suit to my skin. HURRY UP, MAN, HURRY.

Quite suddenly he straightened out, so fast I almost lost him by continuing to turn. I caught him a second later and saw his left hand flash the "dive" signal to me. Then he dipped toward the fog bank; I followed, and we were in it, a shallow, flat descent, but a descent nevertheless, and from a mere hundred feet, toward nothing.

To pass out of even dimly lit sky into cloud or fog is like passing into a bath of gray cotton wool. Suddenly there is nothing but the gray, whirling strands, a million tendrils reaching out to trap and strangle you, each one touching the cockpit cover with a quick caress, then disappearing back into nothingness. The visibility was down to near zero, no shape, no size, no form, no substance. Except that off my left wing tip, now only forty feet away,

was the form of a Mosquito flying with absolute certainty toward something I could not see. Only then did I realize he was flying without lights. For a second I was amazed, horrified by my discovery; then I realized the wisdom of the man. Lights in fog are treacherous, hallucinatory, mesmeric. You can get attracted to them, not knowing whether they are forty or a hundred feet away from you. The tendency is to move toward them; for two aircraft in the fog, one flying formation on the other, that could spell disaster. The man was right.

Keeping formation with him, I knew he was slowing down, for I, too, was easing back the

throttle, dropping and slowing. In a fraction of a second I flashed a glance at the two instruments I needed; the altimeter was reading zero, so was the fuel gauge, and neither was even flickering. The air-speed indicator, which I had also seen, read 120 knots—and this damn coffin was going to fall out of the sky at 95.

Without warning the shepherd pointed a single forefinger at me, then forward through the windscreen. It meant, "There you are, fly on and land." I stared forward through the now streaming windshield. Nothing. Then, yes, something. A blur to the left, another to the right, then two, one on each

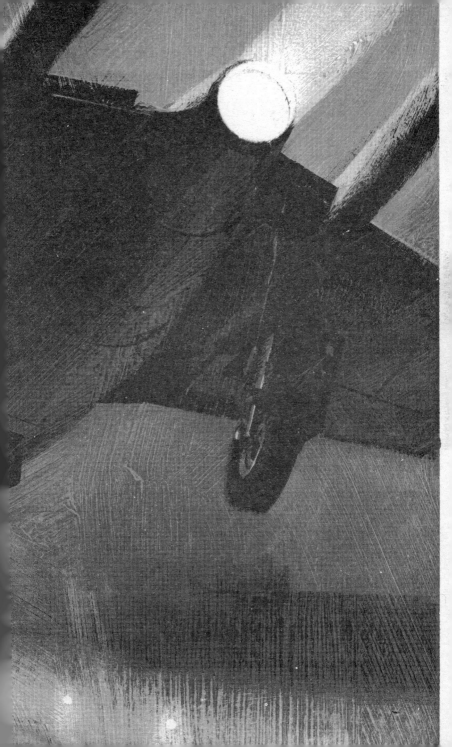

side. Ringed with haze, there were lights on either side of me, in pairs, flashing past. I forced my eyes to see what lay between them. Nothing, blackness. Then a streak of paint running under my feet. The center line. Frantically I closed down the power and held her steady, praying for the Vampire to settle.

The lights were rising now, almost at eye level, and still she would not settle. Bang. We touched, we touched the flaming deck. Bang-bang. Another touch, she was drifting again, inches above the wet black runway. Bam-bam-bam-babam-rumble. She was down; the main wheels had stuck and held.

The Vampire was rolling, at over ninety miles an hour, through a sea of gray fog. I touched the brakes and the nose slammed down onto the deck also. Slow pressure now, no skidding, hold her straight against the skid, more pressure on those brakes or we'll run off the end. The lights moving past more leisurely now, slowing, slower, slower....

The Vampire stopped. I found both of my hands clenched round the control column, squeezing the brake lever inward. I forget now how many seconds I held them there before I would believe we were stopped. Finally, I did believe it, put on the parking brake and released the main brake. Then I went to turn off the engine, for there was no use trying to taxi in this fog; they would have to tow the fighter

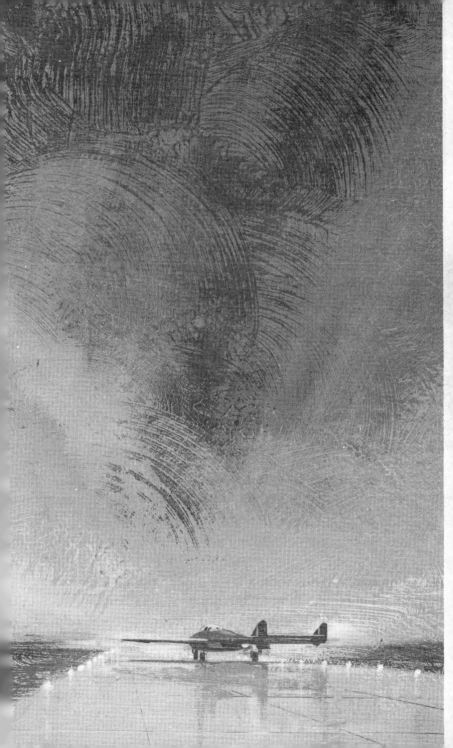

back with a Land-Rover. There was no need to turn
off the engine; it had finally run out of fuel as the
Vampire careered down the runway. I shut off the
remaining systems—fuel, hydraulics, electrics and
pressurization—and slowly began to unstrap myself
from the seat and parachute/dinghy pack. As I did
so, a movement caught my eye. To my left, through
the fog, no more than fifty feet away, low on the
ground with wheels up, the Mosquito roared past
me. I caught the flash of the pilot's hand in the side
window, then he was gone, up into the fog, before he
could see my answering wave of acknowledgment.
But I'd already decided to call up RAF Gloucester

and thank him personally from the officers' mess.

With the systems off, the cockpit was misting up fast, so I released the canopy and wound the hood backward by hand until it locked. Only then, as I stood up, did I realize how cold it was. Against my heated body, dressed in a light nylon flying suit, it was freezing. I expected the control tower truck to be alongside in seconds, for, with an emergency landing, even on Christmas Eve, the fire truck, ambulance and half a dozen other vehicles were always standing by. Nothing happened. At least not for ten minutes.

By the time the two headlights came groping out

of the mist, I felt frozen. The lights stopped twenty feet from the motionless Vampire, dwarfed by the fighter's bulk. A voice called, "Hallo there."

I stepped out of the cockpit, jumped from the wing to the tarmac, and ran toward the lights. They turned out to be the headlamps of a battered old Jowett Javelin. Not an Air Force identification mark in sight. At the wheel of the car was a puffed, beery face and a handlebar moustache. At least he wore an RAF officer's cap. He stared at me as I loomed out of the fog.

"That yours?" He nodded toward the dim shape of the Vampire.

"Yes," I said. "I just landed it."

"'Straordinary," he said, "quite 'straordinary. You'd better jump in. I'll run you back to the mess."

I was grateful for the warmth of the car, even more so to be alive.

Moving in bottom gear, he began to ease the old car back round the taxi track, evidently toward the control tower and, beyond it, the mess buildings. As we moved away from the Vampire, I saw that I had stopped twenty feet short of a plowed field at the very end of the runway.

"You were damned lucky," he said, or rather shouted, for the engine was roaring in first gear and he seemed to be having trouble with the foot

controls. Judging by the smell of whisky on his breath, that was not surprising.

"Damned lucky," I agreed. "I ran out of fuel just as I was landing. My radio and all the electrical systems failed nearly fifty minutes ago over the North Sea."

He spent several minutes digesting the information carefully.

"'Straordinary," he said at length. "No compass?"

"No compass. Flying in the approximate direction by the moon. As far as the coast, or where I judged it to be. After that..."

"No radio?"

"No radio," I said. "A dead box on all channels."

"Then how did you find this place?" he asked.

I was losing patience. The man was evidently one of those passed-over flight lieutenants, not terribly bright and probably not a flier, despite the handlebar moustache. A ground wallah. And drunk with it. Shouldn't be on duty at all on an operational station at that hour of the night.

"I was guided in," I explained patiently. The emergency procedures, having worked so well, now began to seem run-of-the-mill; such is the recuperation of youth. "I flew short, left-hand triangles, as per instructions, and they sent up a shepherd aircraft to guide me down. No problem."

He shrugged, as if to say "If you insist." Finally, he said: "Damned lucky, all the same. I'm surprised the other chap managed to find the place."

"No problem there," I said. "It was one of the weather aircraft from RAF Gloucester. Obviously, he had radio. So we came in here in formation, on a GCA. Then, when I saw the lights at the threshold of the runway, I landed myself."

The man was obviously dense, as well as drunk.

"'Straordinary," he said, sucking a stray drop of moisture off his handlebar. "We don't have GCA. We don't have any navigational equipment at all, not even a beacon."

Now it was my turn to let the information sink in.

"This isn't RAF Merriam St. George?" I asked in a small voice.

He shook his head.

"Marham? Chicksands? Lakenheath?"

"No," he said, "this is RAF Minton."

"I've never heard of it," I said at last.

"I'm not surprised. We're not an operational station. Haven't been for years. Minton's a storage depot. Excuse me."

He stopped the car and got out. I saw we were standing a few feet from the dim shape of a control tower adjoining a long row of Nissen huts, evidently

once flight rooms, navigational and briefing huts. Above the narrow door at the base of the tower through which the officer had disappeared hung a single naked bulb. By its light I could make out broken windows, padlocked doors, an air of abandonment and neglect. The man returned and climbed shakily back behind the wheel.

"Just turning the runway lights off," he said, and belched.

My mind was whirling. This was mad, crazy, illogical. Yet there had to be a perfectly reasonable explanation.

"Why did you switch them on?" I asked.

"It was the sound of your engine," he said. "I was in the officers' mess having a noggin, and old Joe suggested I listen out the window for a second. There you were, circling right above us. You sounded damn low, almost as if you were going to come down in a hurry. Thought I might be of some use, remembered they never disconnected the old runway lights when they dismantled the station, so I ran down to the control tower and switched them on."

"I see," I said, but I didn't. But there had to be an explanation.

"That was why I was so late coming out to pick

you up. I had to go back to the mess to get the car out, once I'd heard you land out there. Then I had to find you. Bloody foggy night."

You can say that again, I thought. The mystery puzzled me for another few minutes. Then I hit on the explanation.

"Where is RAF Minton, exactly?" I asked him.

"Five miles in from the coast, inland from Cromer. That's where we are," he said.

"And where's the nearest operational RAF station with all the radio aids, including GCA?"

He thought for a minute.

"Must be Merriam St. George," he said. "They must have all those things. Mind you, I'm just a stores johnny."

That was the explanation. My unknown friend in the weather plane had been leading me straight in from the coast to Merriam St. George. By chance, Minton, abandoned old stores depot Minton, with its cobwebbed runway lights and drunken commanding officer, lay right along the in-flight path to Merriam's runway. Merriam's controller had asked us to circle twice while he switched on his runway lights ten miles ahead, and this old fool had switched on his lights as well. Result: Coming in on the last ten-mile stretch, I had plonked my Vampire down onto the wrong airfield. I was about to tell

him not to interfere with modern procedures that he couldn't understand when I choked the words back. My fuel had run out halfway down the runway. I'd never have made Merriam, ten miles away. I'd have crashed in the fields short of touch-down. By an amazing fluke I had been, as he said, damned lucky.

By the time I had worked out the rational explanation for my presence at this nearly aban-doned airfield, we had reached the officers' mess. My host parked his car in front of the door and we climbed out. Above the entrance hall a light was burning, dispelling the fog and illuminating the

carved but chipped crest of the Royal Air Force above the doorway. To one side was a board screwed to the wall. It read RAF STATION MINTON. To the other side was another board, announcing OFFICERS' MESS. We walked inside.

The front hall was large and spacious, but evidently built in the prewar years when metal window frames, service issue, were in fashion. The place reeked of the expression "It has seen better days." It had, indeed. Only two cracked-leather club chairs occupied the anteroom, which could have taken twenty. The cloakroom to the right contained a long empty rail for nonexistent coats.

My host, who told me he was Flight Lieutenant Marks, shrugged off his sheepskin coat and threw it over a chair. He was wearing his uniform trousers but with a chunky blue pullover for a jacket. It must be miserable to spend your Christmas on duty in a dump like this.

He told me he was the second-in-command, the C.O. being a squadron leader now on Christmas leave. Apart from him and his C.O., the station boasted a sergeant, three corporals, one of whom was on Christmas duty and presumably in the corporals' mess also on his own, and twenty stores clerks, all away on leave. When not on leave, they

spent their days classifying tons of surplus clothing, parachutes, boots and other impedimenta that go to make up a fighting service.

There was no fire in the vestibule, though there was a large brick fireplace, nor any in the bar, either. Both rooms were freezing cold, and I was beginning to shiver again after recovering in the car. Marks was putting his head through the various doors leading off the hall, shouting for someone called Joe. By looking through after him, I took in at a glance the spacious but deserted dining room, also fireless and cold, and the twin passages, one leading to the officers' private rooms, the other to the staff quarters. RAF messes do not vary much in architecture; once a pattern, always a pattern.

"I'm sorry it's not very hospitable, old boy," said Marks, having failed to find the absent Joe. "Being only the two of us on station here, and no visitors to speak of, we've each made two bedrooms into a sort of self-contained apartment where we live. Hardly seems worth using all this space just for the two of us. You can't heat it in winter, you know; not on the fuel they allow us. And you can't get the staff."

It seemed sensible. In his position, I'd probably have done the same.

"Not to worry," I said, dropping my flying helmet and attached oxygen mask onto the other leather chair in the anteroom. "Though I could do with a bath and a meal."

"I think we can manage that," he said, trying hard to play the genial host. "I'll get Joe to fix up one of the spare rooms—God knows we have enough of them—and heat up the water. He'll also rustle up a meal. Not much, I'm afraid. Bacon and eggs do?"

I nodded. By this time I presumed old Joe was the mess steward.

"That will do fine. While I'm waiting, do you mind if I use your phone?"

"Certainly, certainly, of course, you'll have to check in."

He ushered me into the mess secretary's office, through a door beside the entrance to the bar. It was small and cold, but it had a chair, an empty desk and a telephone. I dialed 100 for the local operator and while I was waiting, Marks returned with a tumbler of whisky. Normally, I hardly touch spirits, but it was warming, so I thanked him and he went off to supervise the steward. My watch told me it was close to midnight. Hell of a way to spend Christmas, I thought. Then I recalled how, thirty minutes earlier, I had been crying to God for a bit of help, and felt ashamed.

"Little Minton," said a drowsy voice. It took ages

to get through, for I had no telephone number for Merriam St. George, but the girl got it eventually. Down the line I could hear the telephone operator's family celebrating in a back room, no doubt the living quarters attached to the village post office. After a few minutes, the phone was ringing.

"RAF Merriam St. George," said a man's voice. Duty sergeant speaking from the guardroom, I thought.

"Duty Controller, Air-Traffic Control, please," I said. There was a pause.

"I'm sorry, sir," said the voice, "may I ask who's calling?"

I gave him my name and rank. Speaking from RAF Minton, I told him.

"I see, sir. But I'm afraid there's no flying tonight, sir. No one on duty in Air-Traffic Control. A few of the officers up in the mess, though."

"Then give me the Station Duty Officer, please."

When I got through to him, he was evidently in the mess, for the sound of lively talk could be heard behind him. I explained about the emergency and the fact that his station had been alerted to receive a Vampire fighter coming in on an emergency GCA without radio. He listened attentively. Perhaps he was young and conscientious, too, for he was quite sober, as a station duty officer is supposed to be at all times, even Christmas.

"I don't know about that," he said at length. "I don't think we've been operational since we closed down at five this afternoon. But I'm not on Air-Traffic. Would you hold on? I'll get the wing commander—flying. He's here."

There was a pause and then an older voice came on the line.

"Where are you speaking from?" he said, after noting my name, rank and the station at which I was based.

"RAF Minton, sir. I've just made an emergency

landing here. Apparently, it's nearly abandoned."

"Yes, I know," he drawled. "Damn bad luck. Do you want us to send a Tilly for you?"

"No, it's not that, sir. I don't mind being here. It's just that I landed at the wrong airfield. I believe I was heading for your airfield on a ground-controlled approach."

"Well, make up your mind. Were you or weren't you? You ought to know. According to what you say, you were flying the damn thing."

I took a deep breath and started at the beginning.

"So you see, sir, I was intercepted by the weather plane from Gloucester and he brought me in. But in this fog it must have been on a GCA. No other way to get down. Yet when I saw the lights of Minton, I landed here, assuming it to be Merriam St. George."

"Splendid," he said at length. "Marvelous bit of flying by that pilot from Gloucester. 'Course, those chaps are up in all weathers. It's their job. What do you want us to do about it?"

I was getting exasperated. Wing commander he might have been, but he had had a skinful this Christmas Eve.

"I am ringing to alert you to stand down your radar and traffic-control crews, sir. They must be waiting for a Vampire that's never going to arrive. It's already arrived—here at Minton."

"But we're closed down," he said. "We shut all the systems down at five o'clock. There's been no call for us to turn out."

"But Merriam St. George has a GCA," I protested.

"I know we have," he shouted back. "But it hasn't been used tonight. It's been shut down since five o'clock."

I asked the next and last question slowly and carefully.

"Do you know, sir, where is the nearest RAF station that will be manning one-twenty-one-point-five-megacycle band throughout the night, the nearest station to here that maintains twenty-four-hour emergency listening?" The international aircraft-emergency frequency is 121.5 megacycles.

"Yes," he said equally slowly. "To the west, RAF Marham. To the south, RAF Lakenheath. Good night to you. Happy Christmas."

I put the phone down and sat back and breathed deeply. Marham was forty miles away on the other side of Norfolk. Lakenheath was forty miles to the south, in Suffolk. On the fuel I was carrying, not only could I not have made Merriam St. George, it wasn't even open. So how could I ever have got to

Marham or Lakenheath? And I had told that Mosquito pilot that I had only five minutes' fuel left. He had acknowledged that he understood. In any case, he was flying far too low after we dived into the fog ever to fly forty miles like that. The man must have been mad.

It began to dawn on me that I didn't really owe my life to the weather pilot from Gloucester, but to Flight Lieutenant Marks, beery, bumbling old passed-over Flight Lieutenant Marks, who couldn't tell one end of an aircraft from another but who had run four hundred yards through the fog to switch on the lights of an abandoned runway because he heard a jet engine circling overhead too close to the ground. Still, the Mosquito must be

back at Gloucester by now and he ought to know that, despite everything, I was alive.

"Gloucester?" said the operator. "At this time of night?"

"Yes," I replied firmly, "Gloucester, at this time of night."

One thing about weather squadrons, they're always on duty. The duty meteorologist took the call. I explained the position to him.

"I'm afraid there must be some mistake, Flying Officer," he said. "It could not have been one of ours."

"This *is* RAF Gloucester, right?"

"Yes, it is. Duty Officer speaking."

"Fine. And your unit flies Mosquitoes to take

pressure and temperature readings at altitude, right?"

"Wrong," he said. "We used to use Mosquitoes. They went out of service three months ago. We now use Canberras."

I sat holding the telephone, staring at it in disbelief. Then an idea came to me.

"What happened to them?" I asked. He must have been an elderly boffin of great courtesy and patience to tolerate darn-fool questions at that hour.

"They were scrapped, I think, or sent off to museums, more likely. They're getting quite rare nowadays, you know."

"I know," I said. "Could one of them have been sold privately?"

"I suppose it's possible," he said at length. "It would depend on Air Ministry policy. But I think they went to aircraft museums."

"Thank you. Thank you very much. And Happy Christmas."

I put the phone down and shook my head in bewilderment. What a night, what an incredible night! First I lose my radio and all my instruments, then I get lost and short of fuel, then I am taken in tow by some moonlighting harebrain with a pas-

sion for veteran aircraft flying his own Mosquito through the night, who happens to spot me, comes within an inch of killing me, and finally a half-drunk ground-duty officer has the sense to put his runway lights on in time to save me. Luck doesn't come in much bigger slices. But one thing was certain; that amateur air ace hadn't the faintest idea what he was doing. On the other hand, where would I be without him? I asked myself. Bobbing around dead in the North Sea by now.

I raised the last of the whisky to him and his strange passion for flying privately in outdated aircraft and tossed the drink down. Flight Lieutenant Marks put his head through the doorway.

"Your room's ready," he said. "Number seventeen, just down the corridor. Joe's making up a fire for you. The bath water's heating. If you don't mind, I think I'll turn in. Will you be all right on your own?"

I greeted him with more friendliness than last time, which he deserved.

"Sure, I'll be fine. Many thanks for all your help."

I took my helmet and wandered down the corridor, flanked with the numbers of the bedrooms of bachelor officers long since posted elsewhere. From the doorway of seventeen, a bar of light shone out into the passage. As I entered the room an old

man rose from his knees in front of the fireplace. He gave me a start. Mess stewards are usually RAF enlisted men. This one was near seventy and obviously a locally recruited civilian employee.

"Good evening, sir," he said. "I'm Joe, sir. I'm the mess steward."

"Yes, Joe, Mr. Marks told me about you. Sorry to cause you so much trouble at this hour of the night. I just dropped in, as you might say."

"Yes, Mr. Marks told me. I'll have your room ready directly. Soon as this fire burns up, it'll be quite cozy."

The chill had not been taken off the room and I shivered in the nylon flying suit. I should have

asked Marks for the loan of a sweater but had forgotten.

I elected to take my lonely evening meal in my room, and while Joe went to fetch it, I had a quick bath, for the water was by then reasonably hot. While I toweled myself down and wrapped round me the old but warm dressing gown that old Joe had brought with him, he set out a small table and placed a plate of sizzling bacon and eggs on it. By then the room was comfortably warm, the coal fire burning brightly, the curtains drawn. While I ate, which took only a few minutes, for I was ravenously hungry, the old steward stayed to talk.

"You been here long, Joe?" I asked him, more out

of politeness than genuine curiosity.

"Oh, yes, sir, nigh on twenty years; since just before the war, when the station opened."

"You've seen some changes, eh? Wasn't always like this."

"That it wasn't, sir, that it wasn't." And he told me of the days when the rooms were crammed with eager young pilots, the dining room noisy with the clatter of plates and cutlery, the bar roaring with bawdy songs; of months and years when the sky above the airfield crackled and snarled to the sound of piston engines driving planes to war and bringing them back again.

While he talked I emptied the remainder of the half-bottle of red wine he had brought from the bar store. A very good steward was Joe. After finishing, I rose from the table, fished a cigarette from the pocket of my flying suit, lit it and sauntered round the room. The steward began to tidy up the plates and the glass from the table. I halted before an old photograph in a frame standing alone on the mantel above the crackling fire. I stopped with my cigarette half-raised to my lips, feeling the room go suddenly cold.

The photo was old and stained, but behind its glass it was still clear enough. It showed a young

man of about my own years, in his early twenties, dressed in flying gear. But not the gray suits and gleaming plastic crash helmet of today. He wore thick sheepskin-lined boots, rough serge trousers and a heavy sheepskin zip-up jacket. From his left hand dangled one of the soft-leather flying helmets they used to wear, with goggles attached, instead of the modern pilot's tinted visor. He stood with legs apart, right hand on hip, a defiant stance, but he was not smiling. He stared at the camera with grim intensity. There was something sad about the eyes.

Behind him, quite clearly visible, stood his aircraft. There was no mistaking the lean, sleek silhouette of the Mosquito fighter-bomber, nor the two

low-slung pods housing the twin Merlin engines that gave it its remarkable performance. I was about to say something to Joe when I felt the gust of cold air on my back. One of the windows had blown open and the icy air was rushing in.

"I'll close it, sir," the old man said, and made to put all the plates back down again.

"No, I'll do it."

It took me two strides to cross to where the window swung on its steel frame. To get a better hold, I stepped inside the curtain and stared out. The fog swirled in waves round the old mess building, disturbed by the current of warm air coming from the window. Somewhere, far away in the fog, I thought I heard the snarl of engines. There were no engines out there, just a motorcycle of some farm boy, taking leave of his sweetheart across the fens. I closed the window, made sure it was secure and turned back into the room.

"Who's the pilot, Joe?"

"The pilot, sir?"

I nodded toward the lonely photograph on the mantel.

"Oh, I see, sir. That's a photo of Mr. John Kavanagh. He was here during the war, sir."

He placed the wineglass on top of the topmost plate.

"Kavanagh?" I walked back to the picture and studied it closely.

"Yes, sir. An Irish gentleman. A very fine man, if I may say so. As a matter of fact, sir, this was his room."

"What squadron was that, Joe?" I was still peering at the aircraft in the background.

"Pathfinders, sir. Mosquitoes, they flew. Very fine pilots, all of them, sir. But I venture to say I believe Mr. Johnny was the best of them all. But then I'm biased, sir. I was his batman, you see."

There was no doubting it. The faint letters on the nose of the Mosquito behind the figure in the photo read JK. Not Jig King, but Johnny Kavanagh.

The whole thing was clear as day. Kavanagh had been a fine pilot, flying with one of the crack squadrons during the war. After the war he'd left the Air Force, probably going into second-hand car dealing, as quite a few did. So he'd made a pile of money in the booming Fifties, probably bought himself a fine country house, and had enough left over to indulge his real passion—flying. Or rather re-creating the past, his days of glory. He'd bought up an old Mosquito in one of the RAF periodic auctions of obsolescent aircraft, refitted it and flew it privately whenever he wished. Not a bad way to spend your spare time, if you had the money.

So he'd been flying back from some trip to Europe, had spotted me turning in triangles above the cloud bank, realized I was stuck and taken me in tow. Pinpointing his position precisely by crossed radio beacons, knowing this stretch of the coast by heart, he'd taken a chance on finding his old airfield at Minton, even in thick fog. It was a hell of a risk. But then I had no fuel left, anyway, so it was that or bust.

I had no doubt I could trace the man, probably through the Royal Aero club.

"He was certainly a good pilot," I said reflectively, thinking of this evening's performance.

"The best, sir," said old Joe from behind me.

"They reckoned he had eyes like a cat, did Mr. Johnny. I remember many's the time the squadron would return from dropping marker flares over bombing targets in Germany and the rest of the young gentlemen would go into the bar and have a drink. More likely several."

"He didn't drink?" I asked.

"Oh, yes, sir, but more often he'd have his Mosquito refueled and take off again alone, going back over the Channel or the North Sea to see if he could find some crippled bomber making for the coast and guide it home."

I frowned. Those big bombers had their own bases to go to.

"But some of them would have taken a lot of enemy flak fire and sometimes they had their radios knocked out. All over, they came from. Marham, Scampton, Waddington; the big four-engined ones, Halifaxes, Stirlings, and Lancasters; a bit before your time, if you'll pardon my saying so, sir."

"I've seen pictures of them," I admitted. "And some of them fly in air parades. And he used to guide them back?"

I could imagine them in my mind's eye, gaping holes in the body, wings, and tail, creaking and swaying as the pilot sought to hold them steady for home, a wounded or dying crew and the radio shot to bits. And I knew, from too recent experience, the bitter loneliness of the winter's sky at night, with no radio, no guide for home, and the fog blotting out the land.

"That's right, sir. He used to go up for a second flight in the same night, patrolling out over the North Sea, looking for a crippled plane. Then he'd guide it home, back here to Minton, sometimes through fog so dense you couldn't see your hand. Sixth sense, they said he had—something of the Irish in him."

I turned from the photograph and stubbed my cigarette butt into the ashtray by the bed. Joe was at the door.

"Quite a man," I said, and I meant it. Even today, middle-aged, he was a superb flier.

"Oh, yes, sir, quite a man, Mr. Johnny. I remember him saying to me once, standing right where you are, before the fire: 'Joe,' he said, 'whenever there's one of them out there in the night, trying to get back, I'll go out and bring him home.'"

I nodded gravely. The old man so obviously worshiped his wartime officer.

"Well," I said, "by the look of it, he's still doing it." Now Joe smiled.

"Oh, I hardly think so, sir. Mr. Johnny went out on his last patrol Christmas Eve 1943, just fourteen years ago tonight. He never came back, sir. He went down with his plane somewhere out there in the North Sea. Good night, sir. And Happy Christmas."

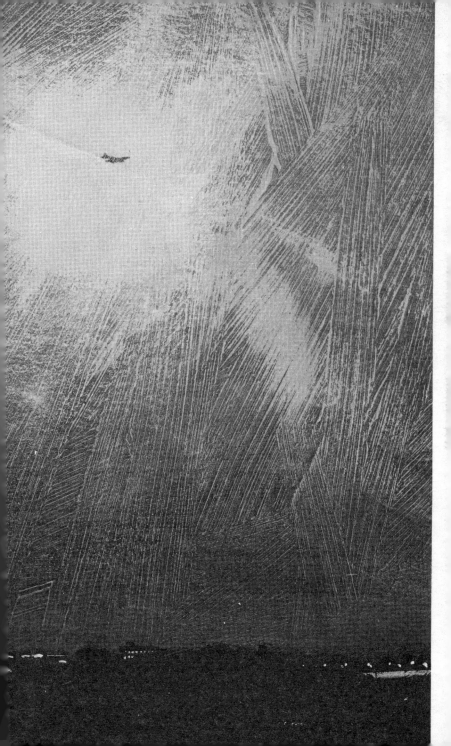

Read on for an excerpt from
Frederick Forsyth's classic thriller

THE DAY OF THE JACKAL

'A book that broke the mould'
LEE CHILD

Available in Arrow Books

arrow books

CHAPTER ONE

It is cold at six-forty in the morning of a March day in Paris, and seems even colder when a man is about to be executed by firing squad. At that hour on 11th March 1963, in the main courtyard of the Fort d'Ivry, a French Air Force colonel stood before a stake driven into the chilly gravel as his hands were bound behind the post, and stared with slowly diminishing disbelief at the squad of soldiers facing him twenty metres away.

A foot scuffed the grit, a tiny release from tension, as the blindfold was wrapped around the eyes of Lieutenant-Colonel Jean-Marie Bastien-Thiry, blotting out the light for the last time. The mumbling of the priest was a helpless counterpoint to the crackling of twenty rifle bolts as the soldiers charged and cocked their carbines.

Beyond the walls a Berliet truck blared for a passage as some smaller vehicle crossed its path towards the centre of the city; the sound died away, masking the 'Take your aim' order from the officer in charge of the squad. The crash of rifle fire, when it came, caused no ripple on the surface of the waking city, other than to send a flutter of pigeons skywards for a few moments. The single 'whack' seconds later of the *coup-de-grâce* was lost in the rising din of traffic from beyond the walls.

The death of the officer, leader of a gang of Secret Army Organization killers who had sought to shoot the President of France, was to have been an end – an end to further attempts on the President's life. By a quirk of fate it marked a beginning, and to explain why it must first be necessary to explain why a riddled body came to hang from

1

its ropes in the courtyard of the military prison outside Paris on that March morning . . .

The sun had dropped at last behind the palace wall and long shadows rippled across the courtyard bringing a welcome relief. Even at seven in the evening of the hottest day of the year the temperature was still 23 degrees Centigrade. Across the sweltering city the Parisians piled querulous wives and yelling children into cars and trains to leave for the weekend in the country. It was 22nd August, 1962, the day a few men waiting beyond the city boundaries had decided that the President, General Charles de Gaulle, should die.

While the city's population prepared to flee the heat for the relative cool of the rivers and beaches the Cabinet meeting behind the ornate façade of the Elysée Palace, continued. Across the tan gravel of the front courtyard, now cooling in welcome shadow, sixteen black Citroën DS saloons were drawn up nose to tail, forming a circle round threequarters of the area.

The drivers, lurking in the deepest shade close to the west wall where the shadows had arrived first, exchanged the inconsequential banter of those who spend most of their working days waiting on their masters' whims.

There was more desultory grumbling at the unusual length of the Cabinet's deliberations until a moment before 7.30 a chained and bemedalled usher appeared behind the plate-glass doors at the top of the six steps of the palace and gestured towards the guards. Among the drivers half-smoked Gaulloises were dropped and ground into the gravel. The security men and guards stiffened in their boxes beside the front gate and the massive iron grilles were swung open.

The chauffeurs were at the wheels of their limousines when the first group of Ministers appeared behind the plate glass. The usher opened the doors and the members of the Cabinet straggled down the steps exchanging a few last-minute pleasantries for a restful weekend. In order of precedence the saloons eased up to the base of the steps, the usher opened the rear door with a bow, the Ministers climbed into their respective cars and were driven away past the salutes of the Garde Républicaine and out into the Faubourg St Honoré.

Within ten minutes they were gone. Two long black DS 19 Citroëns remained in the yard, and each slowly cruised to the base of the steps. The first, flying the pennant of the President of the French Republic, was driven by Francis Marroux, a police driver from the training and headquarters camp of the Gendarmerie Nationale at Satory. His silent temperament had kept him apart from the joking of the ministerial drivers in the courtyard; his ice-cold nerves and ability to drive fast and safely kept him De Gaulle's personal driver. Apart from Marroux the car was empty. Behind it the second DS 19 was also driven by a gendarme from Satory.

At 7.45 another group appeared behind the glass doors and again the men on the gravel stiffened to attention. Dressed in his habitual double-breasted charcoal-grey suit and dark tie Charles de Gaulle appeared behind the glass. With old-world courtesy he ushered Madame Yvonne de Gaulle first through the doors, then took her arm to guide her down the steps to the waiting Citroën. They parted at the car, and the President's wife climbed into the rear seat of the front vehicle on the left-hand side. The General got in beside her from the right.

Their son-in-law, Colonel Alain de Boissieu, then Chief of Staff of the armoured and cavalry units of the French Army, checked that both rear doors were safely shut, then took his place in the front beside Marroux.

In the second car two others from the group of functionaries who had accompanied the presidential couple down the steps took their seats. Henri d'Jouder, the hulking bodyguard of the day, a Kabyle from Algeria, took the front seat beside the driver, eased the heavy revolver under his left armpit, and slumped back. From then on his eyes would flicker incessantly, not over the car in front, but over the pavements and street corners as they flashed past. After a last word to one of the duty security men to be left behind, the second man got into the back alone. He was Commissaire Jean Ducret, chief of the Presidential Security Corps.

From beside the west wall two white-helmeted motards gunned their engines into life and rode slowly out of the shadows towards the gate. Before the entrance they stopped ten feet apart and glanced back. Marroux pulled the first Citroën away from the steps, swung towards the gate and drew up behind the motorcycle outriders. The second car followed. It was 7.50 p.m.

Again the iron grille swung open and the small cortège swept past the ramrod guards into the Faubourg St Honoré. Arriving at the end of the Faubourg St Honoré the convoy swept into the Avenue de Marigny. From under the chest-nut trees a young man in a white crash helmet astride a scooter watched the cortège pass, then slid away from the kerb and followed. Traffic was normal for an August weekend and no advance warning of the President's departure had been given. Only the whine of the motor-cycle sirens told traffic cops on duty of the approach of the convoy, and they had to wave and whistle frantically to get the traffic stopped in time.

The convoy picked up speed in the tree-darkened avenue and erupted into the sunlit Place Clemenceau, heading straight across towards the Pont Alexandre III. Riding in the slipstream of the official cars the scooterist had little difficulty in following. After the bridge Marroux followed the motor-cyclists into the Avenue General Gallieni and thence into the broad Boulevard des Invalides. The scooterist at this point has his answer. At the junction of the Boulevard des Invalides and the Rue de Varennes he eased back the screaming throttle and swerved towards a corner café. Inside, taking a small metal token from his pocket, he strode to the back of the café where the telephone was situated and placed a local call.

*   *   *

4

Lieutenant-Colonel Jean-Marie Bastien-Thiry waited in a café in the suburb of Meudon. He was thirty-five, married with three children and he worked in the Air Ministry. Behind the conventional façade of his professional and family life he nurtured a deep bitterness towards Charles de Gaulle, who, he believed, had betrayed France and the men who in 1958 had called him back to power, by yielding Algeria to the Algerian nationalists.

He had lost nothing through the loss of Algeria, and it was not personal consideration that motivated him. In his own eyes he was a patriot, a man convinced that he would be serving his beloved country by slaying the man he thought had betrayed her. Many thousands shared his views at that time, but few in comparison were fanatical members of the Secret Army Organization which had sworn to kill De Gaulle and bring down his government. Bastien-Thiry was such a man.

He was sipping a beer when the call came through. The barman passed him the phone, then went to adjust the television set at the other end of the bar. Bastien-Thiry listened for a few seconds, muttered 'Very good, thank you' into the mouthpiece and set it down. His beer was already paid for. He strolled out of the bar on to the pavement, took a rolled newspaper from under his arm, and carefully unfolded it twice.

Across the street a young woman let drop the lace curtain of her first-floor flat, and turned to the twelve men who lounged about the room. She said, 'It's route number two.' The five youngsters, amateurs at the business of killing, stopped twisting their hands and jumped up.

The other seven were older and less nervous. Senior among them in the assassination attempt and second-in-command to Bastien-Thiry was Lieutenant Alain Bougrenet de la Tocnaye, an extreme right-winger from a family of landed gentry. He was thirty-five, married with two children.

The most dangerous man in the room was Georges Watin, aged thirty-nine, a bulky-shouldered, square-jowled

5

OAS fanatic, originally an agricultural engineer from Algeria, who in two years had emerged again as one of the OAS's most dangerous trigger-men. From an old leg-wound he was known as the Limp.

When the girl announced the news the twelve men trooped downstairs via the back of the building to a side street where six vehicles, all stolen or hired, had been parked. The time was 7.55.

Bastien-Thiry had personally spent days preparing the site of the assassination, measuring angles of fire, speed and distance of the moving vehicles, and the degree of firepower necessary to stop them. The place he had chosen was a long straight road called the Avenue de la Libération, leading up to the main cross-roads of Petit-Clamart. The plan was for the first group containing the marksmen with their rifles to open fire on the President's car some two hundred yards before the cross-roads. They would shelter behind an Estafette van parked by the roadside, beginning their fire at a very shallow angle to the oncoming vehicles to give the marksmen the minimum of lay-off.

By Bastien-Thiry's calculations a hundred and fifty bullets should pass through the leading car by the time it came abreast of the van. With the presidential car brought to a stop, the second OAS group would sweep out of a side road to blast the security police vehicle at close range. Both groups would spend a few seconds finishing off the presidential party, then sprint for the three getaway vehicles in another side street.

Bastien-Thiry himself, the thirteenth of the party, would be the lookout man. By 8.05 the groups were in position. A hundred yards on the Paris side of the ambush Bastien-Thiry stood idly by a bus-stop with his newspaper. Waving the newspaper would give the signal to Serge Bernier, leader of the first commando, who would be standing by the Estafette. He would pass the order to the gunmen spread-eagled in the grass at his feet. Bougrenet de la Tocnaye would drive the car to intercept the security police, with Watin the Limp beside him clutching a submachine gun.

* * *

As the safety catches flicked off beside the road at Petit-Clamart, General de Gaulle's convoy cleared the heavier traffic of central Paris and reached the more open avenues of the suburbs. Here the speed increased to nearly sixty miles per hour.

As the road opened out, Francis Marroux flicked a glance at his watch, sensed the testy impatience of the old General behind him and pushed the speed up even higher. The two motor-cycle outriders dropped back to take up station at the rear of the convoy. De Gaulle never liked such ostentation sitting out in front and dispensed with them whenever he could. In this manner the convoy entered the Avenue de la Division Leclerc at Petit-Clamart. It was 8.17 p.m.

A mile up the road Bastien-Thiry was experiencing the effects of his big mistake. He would not learn of it until told by the police as he sat months later in Death Row. Investigating the timetable of his assassination he had consulted a calendar to discover that dusk fell on 22nd August at 8.35, seemingly plenty late enough even if De Gaulle was late on his usual schedule, as indeed he was. But the calendar the Air Force colonel had consulted related to 1961. On 22nd August, 1962, dusk fell at 8.10. Those twenty-five minutes were to change the history of France. At 8.18 Bastien-Thiry discerned the convoy hurtling down the Avenue de la Libération towards him at seventy miles per hour. Frantically he waved his newspaper.

Across the road and a hundred yards down, Bernier peered angrily through the gloom at the dim figure by the bus stop. 'Has the Colonel waved his paper yet?' he asked of no one in particular. The words were hardly out of his mouth when he saw the shark nose of the President's car flash past the bus-stop and into vision. 'Fire!' he screamed to the men at his feet. They opened up as the convoy came abreast of them, firing with a ninety-degree lay-off at a moving target passing them at seventy miles per hour.

That the car took twelve bullets at all was a tribute to

7

the killers' marksmanship. Most of those hit the Citroën from behind. Two tyres shredded under the fire, and although they were self-sealing tubes the sudden loss of pressure caused the speeding car to lurch and go into a front-wheel skid. That was when Francis Marroux saved De Gaulle's life.

While the ace marksman, ex-legionnaire Varga cut up the tyres, the remainder emptied their magazines at the disappearing rear window. Several slugs passed through the bodywork and one shattered the rear window, passing within a few inches of the presidential nose. In the front seat Colonel de Boissieu turned and roared 'Get down' at his parents-in-law. Madame de Gaulle lowered her head towards her husband's lap. The General gave vent to a frosty 'What, again?' and turned to look out of the back window.

Marroux held the shuddering steering wheel and gently turned into the skid, easing down the accelerator as he did so. After a momentary loss of power the Citroën surged forward again towards the intersection with the Avenue du Bois, the side road where the second commando of OAS men waited. Behind Marroux the security car clung to his tail, untouched by any bullets at all.

For Bougrenet de la Tocnaye, waiting with engine running in the Avenue du Bois, the speed of the approaching cars gave him a clear choice: to intercept and commit suicide as the hurtling metal cut him to pieces or let the clutch in a half-second too late. He chose the latter. As he swung his car out of the side road and into line with the presidential convoy, it was not De Gaulle's car he came alongside, but that of the marksman bodyguard d'Jouder and Commissaire Ducret.

Leaning from the right-hand side window, outside the car from the waist up, Watin emptied his submachine gun at the back of the DS in front, in which he could see De Gaulle's haughty profile through the smashed glass.

'Why don't those idiots fire back?' De Gaulle asked plaintively. D'Jouder was trying to get a shot at the OAS killers across ten feet of air between the two cars, but the police driver blocked his view. Ducret shouted to the driver to stick with the President, and a second later the OAS were left behind. The two motor-cycle outriders, one having nearly been unseated by de la Tocnaye's sudden rush out of the side road, recovered and closed up. The whole convoy swept into the roundabout and road junction, crossed it, and continued towards Villacoublay.

At the ambush site the OAS men had no time for recriminations. These were to come later. Leaving the three cars used in the operation they leapt aboard the getaway vehicles and disappeared into the descending gloom.

From his car-borne transmitter Commissaire Ducret called Villacoublay and told them briefly what had happened. When the convoy arrived ten minutes later General de Gaulle insisted on driving straight to the apron where the helicopter was waiting. As the car stopped, a surge of officers and officials surrounded it, pulling open the doors to assist a shaken Madame de Gaulle to her feet. From the other side the General emerged from the debris and shook glass splinters from his lapel. Ignoring the panicky solicitations from the surrounding officers, he walked round the car to take his wife's arm.

'Come, my dear, we are going home,' he told her, and finally gave the Air Force staff his verdict on the OAS. 'They can't shoot straight.' With that he guided his wife into the helicopter and took his seat beside her. He was joined by d'Jouder and they took off for a week-end in the country.

On the tarmac Francis Marroux sat ashen-faced behind the wheel still. Both tyres along the right-hand side of the car had finally given out and the DS was riding on its rims. Ducret muttered a quiet word of congratulation to him, then went on with the business of clearing up.

The Day of the Jackal

Frederick Forsyth

'A book that broke the mould' LEE CHILD

One of the most celebrated thrillers ever written, *The Day of the Jackal* is the electrifying story of the struggle to catch a killer before it's too late.

It is 1963 and an anonymous Englishman has been hired by the Operations Chief of the O.A.S. to murder General de Galle. A failed attempt in the previous year means the target will be nearly impossible to get to. But this latest plot involves a lethal weapon: an assassin of legendary talent.

Known only as The Jackal this remorseless and deadly killer must be stopped, but how do you track a man who exists in name alone?

'In a class by itself. Unputdownable'
Sunday Times

'I was spellbound . . . riveted by this chilling story.'
Guardian

arrow books

ALSO AVAILABLE IN ARROW

The Dogs of War

Frederick Forsyth

An astonishing discovery is made in the remote African republic of Zangaro, one which could change the course of a nation's history forever. But such a discovery cannot be kept secret for long and Sir James Manson will stop at nothing to protect this find. A ruthless and bloody-minded tycoon, Manson immediately hires an army of mercenaries and with this deadly crew behind him he sets out to topple the government and replace its dictator with a puppet president.

But news of the discovery has reached Russia – and suddenly Manson finds he no longer makes the rules in this power game. A game in which win or lose means life or death.

'Enormous and convincing detail, and a shattering climax'
Sunday Mirror

arrow books

The Devil's Alternative

Frederick Forsyth

'Whichever option I choose, men are going to die.'

When the entire Soviet Union wheat crop is destroyed by a devastating string of failures the population faces starvation. The USA is quick to offer assistance. They devise a plan to trade vital food resources with the Russians in exchange for sensitive political information. But the Politburo has other ideas: the invasion of Western Europe to commandeer the food for themselves . . .

As the paths of communication breakdown the president of the United States and leaders from around the world face an appalling choice: Should they allow the loss of thousands to save the lives of many more? This is the Devil's Alternative and in this incomparable and gripping thriller the Cold War giants must fight a battle to the death.

'Compulsively readable . . . I was hypnotised'
Financial Times

arrow books

ALSO AVAILABLE IN ARROW

The Fourth Protocol

Frederick Forsyth

Plan Aurora, hatched in a remote dacha in the forest outside
Moscow and initiated with relentless brilliance and skill, is a plan
within a plan that, in its spine-chilling ingenuity, breaches the ultra-
secret Fourth Protocol and turns the fears that shaped it into a
living nightmare.

A crack Soviet agent, placed under cover in a quiet English country
town, begins to assemble a jigsaw of devastation. MI5 investigator
John Preston, working against the most urgent of deadlines, leads
an operation to prevent the act of murderous destruction aimed
at tumbling Britain into revolution . . .

'A triumph . . . as good as any Forsyth since the jackal'
The Times

arrow books

Odessa File

Frederick Forsyth

Can you forgive the past?

It's 1963 and a young German reporter has been assigned the suicide of a holocaust survivor. The news story seems straight-forward; this is a tragic insight into one man's suffering. But a long hidden secret is discovered in the pages of the dead man's diary.

What follows is life-and-death hunt for a notorious former concentration camp-commander, a man responsible for the deaths of thousands, a man as yet unpunished.

'Brilliant entertainment and a disquieting book'
Guardian

arrow books

No Comebacks

Frederick Forsyth

Deception, blackmail, murder, revenge – these are the themes of stories that move from London to the coast of Spain, from Mauritius to Dublin to Dordogne. Whether his subject is assassination by stealth, the cruel confidence trick or the cold shock of coincidence, Frederick Forsyth is never less than compulsive, the detail always authentic.

Ten stories with the master's touch – a brilliantly readable first collection by an incomparable craftsman of suspense.

'A diverting collection of short suspense fiction that should be both surprise and delight Forsyth fans'
New York Times Book Review

arrow books

THE POWER OF READING

Visit the Random House website and get connected with information on all our books and authors

EXTRACTS from our recently published books and selected backlist titles

COMPETITIONS AND PRIZE DRAWS Win signed books, audiobooks and more

AUTHOR EVENTS Find out which of our authors are on tour and where you can meet them

LATEST NEWS on bestsellers, awards and new publications

MINISITES with exclusive special features dedicated to our authors and their titles

READING GROUPS Reading guides, special features and all the information you need for your reading group

LISTEN to extracts from the latest audiobook publications

WATCH video clips of interviews and readings with our authors

RANDOM HOUSE INFORMATION including advice for writers, job vacancies and all your general queries answered

Come home to Random House
www.rbooks.co.uk